Bajo las olas/Under the Sea

Manatíes/Manatees

por/by Jody Sullivan Rake

Traducción/Translation: Dr. Martín Luis Guzmán Ferrer
Editor Consultor/Consulting Editor: Dra. Gail Saunders-Smith

Consultor/Consultant: Debbie Nuzzolo, Education Manager
SeaWorld, San Diego, California

Capstone
press®

Mankato, Minnesota

Pebble Plus is published by Capstone Press,
151 Good Counsel Drive, P.O. Box 669, Mankato, Minnesota 56002.
www.capstonepress.com

1 2 3 4 5 6 13 12 11 10 09 08

Library of Congress Cataloging-in-Publication Data
Rake, Jody Sullivan.
   [Manatees. Spanish & English]
   Manatíes / por Jody Sullivan Rake = Manatees / by Jody Sullivan Rake.
   p. cm. — (Pebble Plus. Bajo las olas = Pebble Plus. Under the sea)
   ISBN-13: 978-1-4296-2286-8 (hardcover)
   ISBN-10: 1-4296-2286-5 (hardcover)
   1. Manatees — Juvenile literature. I. Title. II. Series.
QL737.S63R3518 2009
599.55 — dc22   2008001456

Summary: Simple text and photographs present manatees and their lives under the sea — in both English
and Spanish.

Editorial Credits
Martha E. H. Rustad, editor; Katy Kudela, bilingual editor; Eida del Risco, Spanish copy editor; Juliette Peters,
set designer; Patrick D. Dentinger, book designer; Wanda Winch, photo researcher/photo editor

Photo Credits
Bruce Coleman Inc./P & R Hagan, 18–19
Jeff Rotman, 1
Kevin Schafer Photography, 14–15
Minden Pictures/Chris Newbert, cover, 16–17; Fred Bavendam, 8–9, 12–13; Norbert Wu, 20–21
Nature Picture Library/Doug Perrine, 10–11
Tom Stack & Associates, Inc./Brian Parker, 6–7; Tom Stack, 4–5

Note to Parents and Teachers

The Bajo las olas/Under the Sea set supports national science standards related to the
diversity and unity of life. This book describes and illustrates manatees in both English
and Spanish. The images support early readers in understanding the text. The repetition
of words and phrases helps early readers learn new words. This book also introduces
early readers to subject-specific vocabulary words, which are defined in the Glossary
section. Early readers may need assistance to read some words and to use the Table of
Contents, Glossary, Internet Sites, and Index sections of the book.

Manatees

by Jody Sullivan Rake

LG (K-3)
ATOS 1.7
0.5 pts
Non-Fiction

112217 EN

Table of Contents

What Are Manatees?. 4

Body Parts. 8

What Manatees Do 12

Under the Sea. 20

Glossary 22

Internet Sites. 24

Index 24

Tabla de contenidos

¿Qué son los manatíes?. 4

Las partes del cuerpo 8

Lo que hacen los manatíes 12

Bajo las olas. 20

Glosario 23

Sitios de Internet 24

Índice 24

What Are Manatees?

Manatees are water mammals.

They swim in seas and rivers.

¿Qué son los manatíes?

Los manatíes son mamíferos

acuáticos. Los manatíes

nadan en los mares y ríos.

Manatees are about

the size of a large cow.

Manatees are sometimes

called sea cows.

Los manatíes son como del

tamaño de una vaca grande.

A los manatíes algunas veces

se les llama vacas marinas.

Body Parts

Manatees have two flippers.

Manatees hold food up

to their mouths with

their flippers.

Las partes del cuerpo

Los manatíes tienen

dos aletas. Los manatíes

se llevan la comida a

la boca con sus aletas.

Manatees have hundreds
of whiskers. Manatees
feel with their whiskers.

Los manatíes tienen cientos
de bigotes. Los manatíes usan
los bigotes para tocar y palpar.

What Manatees Do

Manatees feel for plants on
the bottom of rivers and
bays. Manatees eat the
plants they find.

Lo que hacen
los manatíes

Los manatíes tocan para encontrar
plantas en el fondo de los ríos y
bahías. Los manatíes se comen
las plantas que encuentran.

Manatees flap their flat tails
up and down to swim.
Manatees swim slowly.

Los manatíes agitan sus colas
planas de arriba hacia abajo
para nadar. Los manatíes
nadan despacito.

Manatees close their nostrils

when they are in the water.

They poke their nostrils out

of the water to breathe air.

Los manatíes cierran las ventanas

de la nariz cuando están dentro

del agua. Los manatíes sacan

las ventanas de la nariz para

respirar el aire.

Manatees listen for low
sounds from other manatees.
Manatees have small ears
that hear the sounds.

Los manatíes escuchan los sonidos
bajitos que hacen otros manatíes.
Los manatíes tienen unas orejas
pequeñas para oír los sonidos.

Under the Sea

Manatees spend their lives

in warm seas and rivers.

Bajo las olas

Los manatíes se pasan toda

su vida en los mares y

los ríos templados.

Glossary

bay — a part of the ocean that is partly closed in by land

flipper — a flat limb with bones; manatees use their flippers to swim and to hold food.

mammal — a warm-blooded animal that breathes air; mammals have hair or fur; female mammals feed milk to their young.

nostril — an opening in a nose through which one breathes air; manatees put their nostrils above the water to breathe air.

river — a large natural stream of fresh water that flows into lakes or oceans; manatees sometimes travel up rivers from the ocean.

whisker — a long hair near the mouth of an animal; manatees use their whiskers to feel for food.

Glosario

la aleta — brazo plano con huesos; los manatíes
usan sus aletas para nadar y llevarse la comida
a la boca.

la bahía — parte del mar parcialmente rodeada
por tierra

el bigote — pelo largo cerca de la boca de
un animal; los manatíes usan sus bigotes para
buscar comida.

el mamífero — animal de sangre caliente con
columna que respira aire con sus pulmones;
los mamíferos tienen piel o pelo; las hembras
de los mamíferos alimentan a sus crías con leche.

el río — gran corriente natural de agua dulce
que fluye a los lagos y mares; algunas veces
los manatíes nadan río arriba desde el mar.

la ventana de la nariz — apertura en la nariz a
través de la cual respiramos; los manatíes colocan
esas ventanas sobre el agua para respirar.

Internet Sites

FactHound offers a safe, fun way to find Internet sites related to this book. All of the sites on FactHound have been researched by our staff.

Here's how:

1. Visit *www.facthound.com*

2. Choose your grade level.

3. Type in this book ID **1429622865** for age-appropriate sites. You may also browse subjects by clicking on letters, or by clicking on pictures and words.

4. Click on the **Fetch It** button.

FactHound will fetch the best sites for you!

Index

bays, 12

breathing, 16

ears, 18

eating, 8, 12

feeling, 10, 12

flippers, 8

hearing, 18

mammals, 4

mouths, 8

nostrils, 16

plants, 12

rivers, 4, 12, 20

sea cows, 6

seas, 4, 20

size, 6

sounds, 18

swimming, 4, 14

tails, 14

whiskers, 10

Sitios de Internet

FactHound te brinda una manera divertida y segura de encontrar sitios de Internet relacionados con este libro. Hemos investigado todos los sitios de FactHound. Es posible que algunos sitios no estén en español.

Se hace así:

1. Visita *www.facthound.com*

2. Elige tu grado escolar.

3. Introduce este código especial **1429622865** para ver sitios apropiados a tu edad, o usa una palabra relacionada con este libro para hacer una búsqueda general.

4. Haz un clic en el botón **Fetch It**.

¡FactHound buscará los mejores sitios para ti!

Índice

aletas, 8

bahías, 12

bigotes, 10

boca, 8

colas, 14

comer, 8, 12

escuchar, 18

mamíferos, 4

mares, 4, 20

nadar, 4, 14

orejas, 18

plantas, 12

respirar, 16

ríos, 4, 12, 20

sonidos, 18

tamaño, 6

tocar, 10, 12

vacas marinas, 6

ventanas de la nariz, 16